3
CONFIDENT
READER

W9-AOA-366

Pig in Love

ISBN 0-7696-4221-7

50395

9 780769 642215

EAN

School Specialty. Publishing

Text Copyright © Vivian French 2005. Illustration Copyright ©
Tim Archbold 2005. First published by Evans Brothers Limited, 2A
Portman Mansions, Chiltern Street, London W1U 6NR, United
Kingdom. This edition published under license from Zero to Ten
Limited. All rights reserved. Printed in China. This edition
published in 2006 by Gingham Dog Press, an imprint of School
Specialty Publishing, a member of the School Specialty Family.

Library of Congress-in-Publication Data is on file with the publisher.

Send all inquiries to:
School Specialty Publishing
8720 Orion Place
Columbus, OH 43240-2111

ISBN 0-7696-4221-7

1 2 3 4 5 6 7 8 9 10 EVN 10 09 08 07 06 05

Pig in Love

By Vivian French
Illustrated by Tim Archbold

Columbus, Ohio

Peter Pig fell in love
with Polly Pig next door.
He took her red roses.

Then, he took her some more.

7

"I love you, Polly Pig.
I hope you love me."

"Why don't we get married?
Please say you agree!"

But Polly said, "No."
She started to cry.

"My father won't let me
until pigs can fly!"

Now, Peter was determined.
So, he made himself wings
out of leather and feathers.

He tied them with string.

Then, he climbed up to the hill
at the edge of the town.

But he couldn't fly up.

He could fly only down.

Then, Cow floated by
in her big, bright balloon.

"Come with me," she yelled.
"I'm off to the moon!"

23

"Oh, yes!" shouted Peter
and Polly together.

"Let's fly to the moon."

"We'll live there forever!"

So, Peter and Polly
flew off and away.

29

Are they happy?
You bet!
And there they will stay.

Challenge Words

agree

determined

forever

Think About It!

1. Did Polly Pig want to marry Peter Pig? Why couldn't she marry him?
2. How did Peter Pig make his wings? Did the wings work?
3. What do you see on pages 31–32 that tells you Peter and Polly are happy?
4. Do you think this story could really happen? Why or why not?
5. This story is set in a rhyme. Read the story again. Point to the words that make the same rhyming sounds.

The Story and You

1. Pretend that you are living on the moon. Describe your surroundings.
2. Have you ever heard the expression "when pigs fly"? What do you think it means?